CAPTAIN TOBY

for
Toby

Text and illustrations copyright © Satoshi Kitamura, 1987

The moral right of the author/illustrator has been asserted

First published in Great Britain 1987 by Blackie Children's Books

This edition first published 1997 by Happy Cat Books, Bradfield,
Essex CO11 2UT

A CIP catalogue record for this book is available from
the British Library

ISBN 1 899248 81 1

Printed in Hong Kong

CAPTAIN TOBY

SATOSHI KITAMURA

Happy Cat Books

One stormy night, Toby was in his bed
listening to the wind.

It roared round the house, tearing at the windows and rattling the doors. It howled so loud that Toby couldn't sleep.

He lay there as the thunder crashed and the rain
pattered on the glass.

Suddenly, he felt the whole house rising and falling.
It was rolling . . .

. . . like a ship in the middle of the ocean.

Captain Toby and his crew were busy
finding their way on the ship's chart.

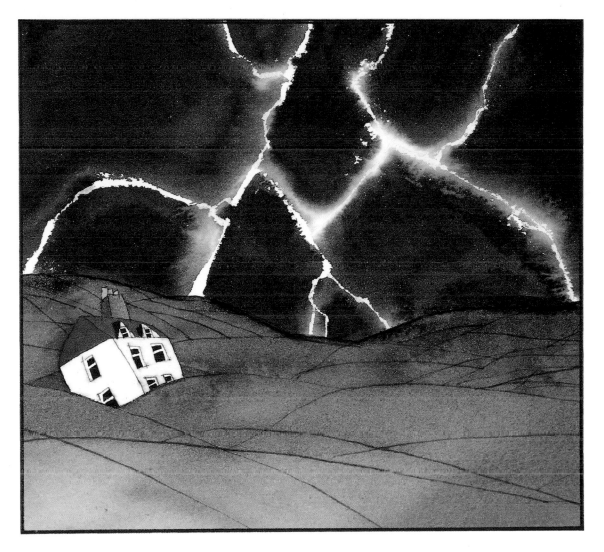

A brilliant flash of lightning lit up the sky.
'There'll be a heavy sea tonight,' said Captain Toby.

All at once, there was a terrific crash. Was it
a rock? Or an enormous wave?

'Hold on!' shouted Captain Toby bravely. He and the crew
rushed to take a look through their binoculars.

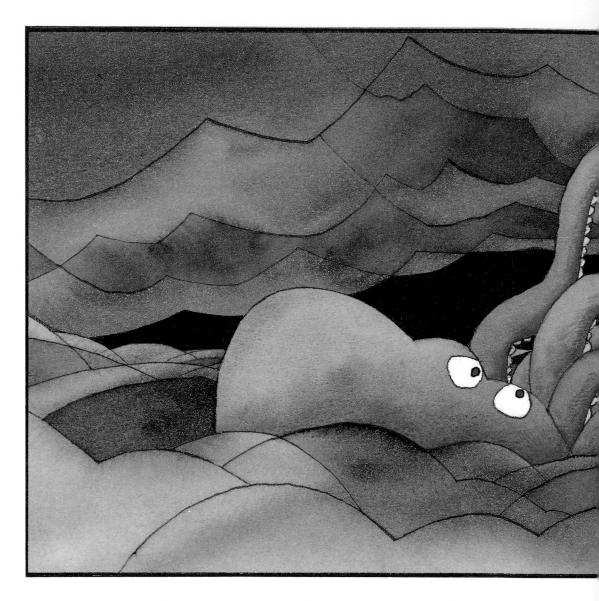

What they saw made Captain Toby shiver.
It was a gigantic octopus!

It was swimming towards them, its terrible
tentacles writhing in all directions.

Captain Toby grabbed the wheel. 'Full steam ahead!'
he cried. 'Aye, aye, sir,' said the crew.

Whatever they did, they could not get up enough speed.
The octopus was getting closer and closer.

Crash! Its horrible tentacles
broke through the window.

'We'll fight,' shouted Captain Toby.
'All night, if we have to.'

But Captain Toby did not know that a submarine
was close at hand. It came speeding to the rescue.

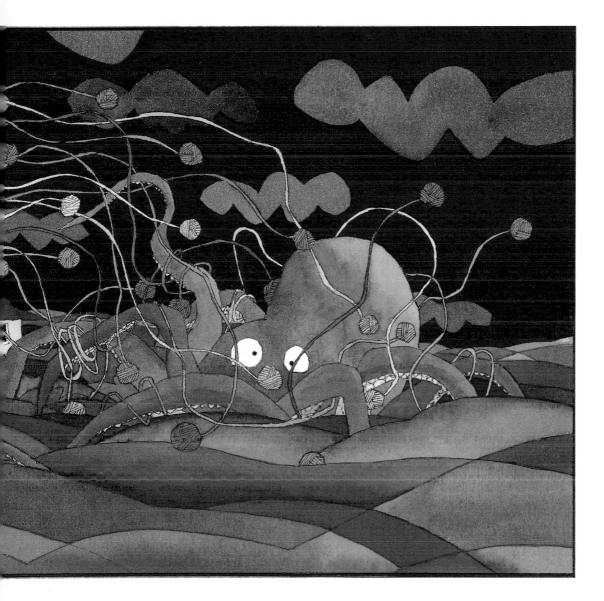

Boom-Boom! Both its guns fired together. The octopus
was so surprised it never knew what hit it!

Captain Grandpa saluted. 'All present and correct?' he shouted.
'Aye, aye,' said Captain Toby. Chief Gunner Grandma smiled.
She never missed a shot.

The seas grew calm and, as the sun rose,
both captains made for harbour.

'I feel like some breakfast,' said Captain Grandpa.
'But there aren't any shops open,' said Chief Gunner Grandma.

Then they saw the octopus.
It was knitting very peacefully.
'Let's not bother it,' said Captain Toby,
'or we'll be late for breakfast.'